MW01180807

# Robinson Hood #3

## CHOPPED

**Jeff Gottesfeld**

SADDLEBACK
EDUCATIONAL PUBLISHING

ROBINSON'S HOOD

THE BANK OF BADNESS

CHOPPED

**SADDLEBACK**
EDUCATIONAL PUBLISHING
www.sdlback.com

ISBN-13: 978-1-62250-002-4
ISBN-10: 1-62250-002-4
eBook: 978-1-61247-686-5

Printed in Guangzhou, China
NOR/1014/CA21401626

18 17 16 15 14   2 3 4 5 6

# Chapter One

It was pitch-black chaos in the storage room.

The gunshots fired by the two Ninth Street Rangers gangstas echoed off the cinder block walls. The gangstas were screaming, crying, and cursing in agony from the pepper spray that fourteen-year-old Robinson "Robin" Paige had just fired at their faces. Off to Robin's left, his friend Karen "Kaykay" Knight was bellowing too. Robin thought she might be shot. As for Robin's ace, Sylvester "Sly" Thomas, Robin heard nothing. He feared his homeboy could be dead, face down on the cold floor in a pool of his own blood.

*Why did we come here*, Robin asked himself. *Why, why, why? I just assed us out. What was I even thinking?*

Robin knew he had just a few seconds to assess, react, and get him and his friends out of the storage yard. Otherwise, the gangstas would fire at them again. The pepper spray wouldn't stop them for long. Only moments stood between him and his friends living or dying.

*That is, if they're even alive.*

But Robin couldn't think. Not only had the gunshots deafened him, but the events of the night also spun willy-nilly through his head like a helicopter with a busted blade.

The decision to come out here, to this storage room where the Ninth Street Rangers kept their drug money and loot. Not to steal money from the Rangers and give it to a righteous cause, but to recover a set of candlesticks that the Rangers had stolen from an old lady friend of his grand-mother's.

Getting through the gate of the U-Store. Picking the Rangers' storage room lock again. Finding the candlesticks that were now in his backpack.

And then the angry voices of the gang-stas as they surprised Robin and his buds. Hitting the floor and killing their flashlight. The click of guns being cocked. Shooting pepper spray at the Rangers at the same time they fired their handguns.

The Rangers screaming.

Kaykay screaming.

It was too much.

Robin forced himself to think. He crawled across the hard concrete. There was Sly!

"You with me?" he hissed.

Sly squeezed Robin's bicep to indicate he was okay. Robin took his homeboy's hand in his and kept crawling. They moved toward the sound of Kaykay's sobs. When they reached her, Robin felt no blood.

"How are you hurt?" He kept his voice low. The Rangers were still cursing and bellowing from the burning pepper spray, but it would be disaster if they heard him and his buds.

*You don't have to be able to see to fire a Glock at a noise*, Robin thought.

"Tried—tried—tried to spray 'em," Kaykay gasped. "Got myself!"

*Oh no*. Kaykay had pepper-sprayed herself by accident. Her face had to feel like it was on fire—eyes tearing crazily, her nose running like a thief in the night.

*But she'll be okay.*

He stood. "Let's get her out of here," he whispered to Sly.

"But the Rangers!" Sly hissed.

"Shut up and do what I do!" Robin hissed back.

He lifted Kaykay to her feet. Sly helped. Then the two boys picked up their friend and crossed to the open door of the storage room. The Rangers weren't there—they'd stepped outside, hollering into the darkness.

Robin realized they could get away, as long as the Rangers didn't see them.

*Gotta move. And fast!*

Kaykay was whimpering. Sly was chubby and out of shape, while Robin was just five feet tall and skinny. But somehow, the two guys half dragged and half carried the panicked Kaykay out of the storage room and toward the gate. The further they got, the heavier Kaykay felt, and the harder it was for her to contain her crying.

"Water!" she gasped. "Gotta wash my eyes! Help me wash out my eyes!"

"Hang in there," Robin told her.

He heard the Rangers' boss screaming in pain again. "Day-um! Day-um! Mah eyes! Mah eyes!"

A few moments later they were outside the yard. Kaykay was really suffering. At least the Rangers hadn't come after them. They had to be suffering too.

"What we gonna do now, guys?" Sly demanded.

"Get her home," Robin said. "Let's get to the bus."

Kaykay moaned. "I can't go home! My parents will kill me! And then they gonna kill you!"

Robin nodded. Kaykay had a point. Her parents would flip if they heard what they'd been doing at the U-Store. Kaykay would be grounded for life and forbidden to hang with Robin and Sly.

There was no time to think about that,

though. If they didn't get out of here, the Rangers could still find them.

*We have pepper spray, and they have Glocks. Ninety-nine times out of a hundred, they win.*

"Come on," he ordered. "Kaykay, we're hauling you again."

Together, Robin and Sly carried her down Decatur Street to the bus stop.

Robin prayed that when they got there, the bus would come before the Rangers did.

***

*At least I've got the candlesticks*, Robin thought grimly as the bus rolled along. He touched his backpack. *Yep. There they are. But we totally blew it otherwise. We had the key to the Rangers' bank of badness. We could've gone back there whenever we wanted to make a "withdrawal." We used their money to save the Center, and we used it to save our school library from closing.*

*Now, they're gonna move their loot some-place else.*

*We'll never find it.*

*I blew it, I blew it, I cold blew it.*

He sighed. At least Kaykay was okay. She sat between Sly and Robin in the back of the bus. They'd found a water bottle under their seat, and after making sure it was water, used it to wash out Kaykay's eyes. That had helped a little. Robin had taken off his hoodie and told Kaykay to blow her streaming nose into it. It was disgusting. He'd have to throw the hoodie away. But at least she wasn't gush-ing snot on herself anymore.

Their plan had been for them each to get home by bus. To clear time for the opera-tion, Robin had lied to his grandmother and said he was studying at the Barbara Jordan Community Center with Kaykay and Sly; Sly's father would drop him home. Kaykay and Sly had told versions of the same story, except with different parents doing the pickup.

The plan had obviously changed. Robin knew they needed some good cover story for why Kaykay was so messed up.

He had it.

As the bus turned onto Marcus Garvey Boulevard, he took Kaykay's cell and pressed Home on her speed dial.

*I dunno if I can get away with this. But I gotta try.*

Mrs. Knight answered. "Hey, baby girl! Everything okay?"

"Hi, Mrs. Knight," Robin tried to keep his voice even. "It's Robin Paige. I'm with Kaykay at the Center, and she's had some kind of allergic reaction to something she ate. I think you need to come get her."

Robin hated to lie, but after nearly dying at the hands of the Rangers, he figured he had a good reason.

"Oh my God! What happened?" Robin heard Mrs. Knight yell for her husband. "Clyde! Get the car! We need to go the Center! And bring me an EpiPen! Kaykay's in trouble."

Too late, Robin remembered that Mrs. Knight was a nurse's aide. He had to be really convincing, now.

"Nah, Mrs. Knight. I think she just needs to get home," Robin invented. "She can breathe fine. It's just that her eyes are swelled and her nose is runny."

"We're on our way," Mrs. Knight promised. "Be there in ten minutes. Do you know what she ate?"

"I think a roll with meat in the center."

"Meat? My baby girl's vegan!"

"She didn't know. Maybe she's allergic to meat now," Robin suggested.

"Don't go anywhere, Robin," Mrs. Knight instructed. "Clyde and I are on our way."

Mrs. Knight clicked off. Robin breathed a little easier as he watched the street signs roll by. The bus passed the scary blocks of Thirtieth Street and Twenty-Eighth Street, which were big drug dealing hangouts—not as dangerous as Robin's own block of Ninth Street, but still plenty dicey. The Center was only five minutes away, now. They'd beat the Knights there for sure.

"You hear that?" Robin asked Kaykay. She was still blowing her nose into his hoodie.

"I heard it. I ate a meat pie." Kaykay's voice was hoarse from wheezing and crying.

"Can you stick to that story?" Robin demanded.

"You have to," Sly told her.

Kaykay nodded. "I can do it." She blew her nose loudly again.

They rode the rest of the way in silence, got off the bus at the Center, and waited for

Kaykay's parents. The Knights got there five minutes after they did, gave Kaykay two useless Benadryls, and loaded her into their old bomber of a car. They didn't question the crazy story about the meat pie allergy.

"Nice lie," Sly told Robin when Kaykay was gone.

Robin nodded. He felt exhausted, as he realized again how close they'd come to dying. All over a pair of candlesticks.

*Never again*, he told himself. *Never, ever again. Sly called our taking money from the bad and giving to the good, "Robin in da hood." As of right now, Robin in da hood is out of business.*

# Chapter Two

Thursday morning, Robin woke up feeling not like he'd been hit by a truck, but by a space shuttle. His whole body hurt. He couldn't figure out why, until he realized his muscles had been so clenched for so long the night before that he was cramping. It took him twice as long as normal to put on his Ironwood Central High School blue uniform and drag himself to school.

He sleepwalked through his morning classes. The ordeal from the night before played over and over in his mind. It also played in his ears—they kept ringing from the gunshots.

Still, he found the energy to go to the library during his study hall. He wanted to help Ms. Herald, the school librarian, get her books back on the shelves. These were the same books that Robin had helped to box up last week when it looked like the school library was going to have to close. Robin was a big reader. The idea that the library was going to close was bad news.

A big donation from the bank of badness saved the library. Their friend from the Center, old Mr. Smith, had pretended that he was giving fifty thousand dollars of his own money. Actually, he was donating Rangers' money.

*And now the bank of badness is closed. Stupid me. Stupid, stupid me!*

Sly and Kaykay came to the library too. It was the one place left at school where they could actually talk because Kaykay was pretending that she hated Robin and Sly and had fallen in love with Tyrone Davis. Tyrone was a Ranger, and Kaykay was actually spying on him to get information about the Rangers for Robin in da hood.

*Of course, there's no need to do that anymore.*

They were confident Tyrone would never set foot in the school library. Or any library, for that matter.

Robin saw Kaykay a few stacks away. He joined her, thinking that for someone who'd inhaled pepper spray the night before, she looked fly. An inch taller than he was, slim, with tawny skin, long dark hair, and hazel eyes. "How you doin'?"

She managed a smile. "Okay. I can see, I can breathe, and I'm alive. Which is saying a lot considering what went down last night."

"I'm sorry about that," Robin told her.

"Don't be." They were in the fiction section, in the *S* area. Kaykay replaced three books by Anne Schraff on the shelf. One was *A Boy Called Twister*, which Robin had liked a lot.

"I almost got us killed!" Robin bent to help her.

"Hey. We tried, we got the sticks, whatchu gonna do?" Kaykay retorted. She had a fast mouth; her words piled up like snow in a blizzard. "The way I see it, I almost got the whole crew killed. Shootin' myself with pepper spray. That's wack! Who does that?"

"Someone scared to death, thas' who."

Robin turned. Sly was at the end of the stack. He wore the same Ironwood Central High School uniform as Robin and Kaykay: blue pants and a light blue shirt.

"You got that right, bro'," Robin agreed. "And I never want to be scared like that again."

Sly made a funny face. "Really, Robin?

Then I suggest you move to Fancyville, 'stead of living here in the hood."

"The worst block in the hood," Kaykay added. She put a few more novels on the shelf.

Robin didn't argue. He did live on the scariest street of the scariest hood in the very scary city of Ironwood. The Rangers dominated Ninth Street. They ran the block with an iron fist, collecting "protection" money from all the businesses.

Robin's grandmother, whom everyone but Robin called Miz Paige, owned a joint on Ninth Street called the Shrimp Shack. Every Friday, the Rangers collected a hundred bucks from her in protection. Protection meant that the Rangers wouldn't torch her shop. Since Robin and his grandma lived in a crappy apartment right above the restaurant, it was important that the shop not go up in flames in the middle of the night.

*We'd get turned into roasted African American marshmallows*, Robin thought grimly. He realized today was Thursday. That meant he would be taking a payoff to the Rangers tomorrow.

Ironwood was a tough city that had seen much better days. Robin and his grandmother were poor, but his friends didn't have it easy, either. Kaykay's mom was a nurse's aide, while her father had been laid off at the auto parts plant and hadn't worked in two years. She had a bunch of brothers and sisters, and her family got SNAP help.

Sly's family did just a little better. His daddy, James "Tex" Thomas, was a preacher, and his mom ran the church music. But it wasn't like the Thomases were rolling in chip. They lived in a small house near Randolph Park. Sly's dream was to be a rich, famous magician in Las Vegas. If he couldn't get that, he'd settle for rich.

"You sayin' Robin in da hood gonna retire?" Sly asked.

"As of last night, we are done. I want to live."

"Word to that," Sly agreed.

"That's all very nice," Kaykay opined. "But who's gonna tell Mr. Smith?"

Robin winced. Mr. Smith was their best friend at the Center and part of Robin in da hood too. He was in his mid-seventies, a retired locksmith whose niece had died in a Rangers' drive-by. Mr. Smith hated the Rangers. When Mr. Smith found out about what happened last night, Robin was sure he would blow a gasket.

"I'll handle it," Robin said reluctantly. He was the leader. It was his responsibility.

"Good luck." Kaykay gave his arm a little squeeze.

Robin liked that. A lot. He and Kaykay had gotten close over the last few weeks. If he didn't have to worry about taking money from gangstas, maybe they could get even closer.

"Let's get back to work," he advised.

They went to different parts of the library. Just in time too. Robin hadn't been away from Sky and Kaykay for two minutes when Tyrone Davis—of all people!—stepped into the library.

"Hey, Shrimp!" Tyrone boomed. "You seen mah super-fine bee-yotch 'round anywhere?"

Robin had been shelving some dictionaries. He fumed at Tyrone calling Kaykay "mah super-fine bee-yotch" like she was a cut of beef at the grocery store.

"Excuse me?" Robin asked.

Tyrone hooted. He was nearly six feet tall, with a soul patch. A former football player, he'd recently started dealing for the Rangers over on Twenty-Eighth Street.

Tyrone had hated Robin forever. He'd nicknamed him "Shrimp" back in fourth grade, both because of Robin's height and because his grandmother ran the Shrimp Shack.

"Oh! Sorry, Shrimp. I meant, you seen mah fine-hot-fly girlfriend, Kay-kay, who used to be your homegirl but done dumped your sorry behind, 'round anywhere?"

Robin grunted. He didn't want to piss Tyrone off too much, since he liked his head attached to his shoulders just the way it was. "I think she's in the fiction section."

"Good! She ain't gonna be there for long! Thanks, Shrimp."

Tyrone bounded toward the back of the library. Robin seethed. That Kaykay had to hang out with this sub-human anymore was just so wrong.

*I gotta put an end to this*, Robin told himself. *But if Tyrone sees her with us, he'll realize we've been playing him. Then the*

*Rangers'll come after us all over again. And who's to say they won't do what they wanted to do last night. Wax us!*

After school, Robin walked home. It took twenty minutes to get from school to Ninth Street. He figured that he'd do his homework and then go help his grandmother in the Shrimp Shack. She had a big party to give on Sunday; there was a lot of prep work. Since Miz Paige had just been released from the hospital after a bout of Lyme disease, Robin knew she could use the help.

Robin's route took him down Marcus Garvey to Ninth Street. Garvey had a lot of car traffic but very few businesses because of all the shootouts and gangbanging that happened on this corner. The only people who ever hung out here were the Rangers' drug sellers.

Today, though, Robin saw a new business was opening. There were a few guys—some white, some black—in mechanics' coveralls painting the garage door. Then, as Robin watched, a late-model sports car—maybe an Audi, maybe a Beemer, Robin didn't know cars that well—pulled up. The guys opened the garage door to admit the sports car, then shut it quickly.

*Huh*. Robin thought this a very odd place for a car repair shop.

*Good luck to them*, he thought. *They're gonna need it.*

# Chapter Three

*Happy birthday to you!*
  *Happy birthday to you!*
  *Happy birthday, Missus Collins!*
  *Happy birthday to you!*

The legal capacity at the Shrimp Shack was sixty-five people. As Robin looked around, there had to be at least that many folks in his grandmother's joint, maybe more. And every one of those sixty-five people joined in for a rousing chorus of "Happy Birthday" for Missus Collins's seventy-fifth birthday.

It was Sunday afternoon. The last few days had been almost normal. The Friday afternoon payoff to the Rangers had gone off without a hitch. Now, Robin, Sly, and Kaykay were helping Robin's grandmother give this birthday party. They'd already served more than a hundred pounds of shrimp.

Missus Collins—she was a tiny woman who wore a pretty flowered dress and fancy hat to her celebration—had a huge family. Doting husband, four daughters, grandchildren, and even a few great-grandchildren. Between her family and friends from church, there was barely room in the Shrimp Shack to move around.

A huge round of applause followed the song. Then Missus Collins tried and failed to blow out seventy-five candles on a giant chocolate cake.

"When you seventy-five, you gonna have a par-tay like this?" Sly asked Robin.

Miz Paige had asked the kids to wear black pants and white shirts to work the party. Sly's sleeves were rolled up as high as they could go.

"You know it," Robin told him. "And you're gonna give it for me at the hotel you're gonna own in Vegas."

Kaykay sidled over. She'd been helping Missus Collins cut her cake. She had on black capri pants and a white men's dress shirt. Robin thought she looked amazing. "Nice party. Know the best part?"

"All the shrimp you ain't eatin'?" Sly jibed.

"Funny." Kaykay shot him a sour look. "Just wait till you're reincarnated in some alternate universe where aliens eat you for lunch. You'll be wishing they were vegan like me."

Sly frowned. "What's 'reincarnated'? And what's an 'alternate universe'?"

Kaykay stared at him, until she realized he was messing with her. All three kids laughed.

"The best part is Tyrone Davis ain't here," she admitted. "He gettin' on my last nerve. What we gonna do 'bout him?"

"Not sure," Robin said. Robin tucked his shirt back into his pants. They couldn't stand around and yak like this for long. Just until everyone had taken a piece of cake.

"You best think of something," Kaykay advised.

"He always does," Sly quipped.

"Well, Tyrone trying to get up into my business, if you know what I'm sayin'," Kaykay reported. "An' I don't want him anywhere near there."

*Ugh.* Robin winced. Kaykay was talking sideways, but it was clear that Tyrone was making moves that involved more than Kaykay's mind and personality. There had to be some way that they could cut Kaykay loose from him. But how? He didn't have an answer.

"Maybe Mr. Smith will know what to do. Hey now, be careful!" Sly edged out of the way of two of Missus Collins's great-grandchildren, who were spinning in circles and trying to walk despite their dizziness. "Did you talk to him yet?"

Robin shook his head. "Nope. Well, I called him. He's sick with a cold and no voice. I figured he should get well before we talk."

Kaykay smiled. "I think you're the one who needs to be well for that convo, Robin Paige."

"No kidding," Robin agreed.

He saw his grandmother across the room motioning for him and his friends to start collecting the empty cake plates. For the next fifteen minutes, the kids were busy on party duty. Then they heard the tinkling of a spoon against a glass.

"Attention please! May I have your attention!"

The voice of Sly's father, Reverend "Tex" Thomas, always commanded respect. The room quieted immediately. Half the people in the room—including Robin's grandmother and Robin—belonged to Reverend Thomas's church. The out-of-towners wished they did.

"I want to make a special announcement and then let the birthday girl say a few words," Reverend Thomas intoned. He was in a suit and tie. He always wore a suit and tie. Robin wanted to ask Sly if his father wore a suit and tie to bed.

"She's my birthday girl!" Missus Collins's husband called out.

Everyone laughed.

"You got that right, Dewayne," Reverend

Thomas agreed. "Missus Collins, would you come stand by me?"

Missus Collins stepped over to Reverend Thomas, who waited until she was at his side to continue. "Missus Collins is a founding member of our church. She still does all the little things that get no glory. Answers phones. Prepares mailings. Visits the sick. Comforts those in mourning. And shows up every Sunday, even in the cold and snow of winter."

"You got that right!" Missus Collins agreed to more laughter. "I got me some good boots!"

Reverend Thomas continued. "I simply want to say that in her honor, I'd like the church to do a charity mission right after Christmas. Down south, where the hurricane hit. There's plenty of good Christian charity to be done with our sweat. If we can raise the money to do the mission, we'll call it the

Collins Mission. In honor of this wonderful woman!" Reverend Thomas took Missus Collins's hand; everyone clapped. "Missus Collins, would you care to say a few words?"

Robin knew what was coming. It gave him a lump in his throat. He edged closer to where Missus Collins was standing so he could see.

"I'm not much on speechifying," the old woman said. "But this week I got a miracle and everyone needs to know it. As you pro'ly know, we got burgled last week. Someone took my great-grandmother's candlesticks, 'mong other things. Those sticks was given to my grandmother on my great-grandma's seventy-fifth birthday and then to my mother when my grandma turned seventy-five. I was planning to give them to my oldest daughter, Denise, today. When they were stolen, I thought that would never happen."

She turned to a small table behind her. On that table were the candlesticks Robin and his friends had retrieved from the Rangers' storage room. Missus Collins showed them to the crowd.

"God works in mysterious ways. Jesus must be watchin' us, because those candlesticks came to me by mail on Friday. No return address. God wanted me to give these to Denise. Thank you, God! Thank you, Jesus!"

The crowd cheered.

"Thank you, Robin."

Robin turned. Kaykay was behind him, whispering to him. She took his hand. He would have fainted with happiness, except for what he saw next.

Mr. Smith. Talking with his gramma over by the counter. They weren't talking like they were strangers, either. They were talking and laughing like they were old friends.

*He's better? He's invited? He knows my grandmother? How? What? Since when?*

"You see that?" Robin asked Kaykay.

Kaykay sniffed. "Hard to miss."

"I gotta talk to him," Robin told her.

"Want me to come with?" Kaykay asked.

He did. He actually wished Kaykay could hear the conversation so they could talk about it afterward. But he shook his head. The right thing to do was talk to Mr. Smith one-to-one. "Nah. I got it covered."

He turned sideways and walked a zigzag through the throng. Mr. Smith, who was now alone, saw him coming and waved happily. "Robin Paige! Or should I say, Robin in da hood?"

"Hi, Mr. Smith," Robin managed. "You feel better already?"

Mr. Smith cleared his throat. " 'Bout eighty percent, which at my age is enough."

Robin decided to start on safer ground than the Ninth Street Rangers. "You know my gramma?"

"I do," Mr. Smith said with a nod.

"Since when?"

"Since before your late daddy was a little boy," Mr. Smith admitted. "Your grandma used to come into my shop now and then. Course, we were all younger then."

Robin was floored. Since his father was a boy? And he didn't know?

"How come you never told me?" It was more an accusation than a question.

Mr. Smith shrugged. "You never asked. It had nothing to do with us. I know Missus Collins too. Two fine ladies. Very fine. Especially your grandmother." Then he shifted. "So, I was thinking … I heard Reverend Thomas talking about the church mission. I'm thinking maybe the Ninth Street Rangers and Robin in da hood can finance that."

*Crap*. Here it was. He had to tell Mr. Smith right now.

He shared the whole story. He didn't try to make himself look better than he was, either.

"I wrecked everything," Robin finished. "The bank of badness is now closed. We can't go back there."

Mr. Smith looked at him, aghast.

"Robin Paige!" He went off on Robin, big time. "I thought you were a smart boy, but you got shrimp for brains! You done blew it! You blew it like a balloon!"

# Chapter Four

Though there was still a birthday party going on, Robin wanted to cry. Mr. Smith was angry with him. Even worse, Mr. Smith was disappointed. Having Mr. Smith disappointed in him was as bad as having his grandmother or his friends disappointed in him.

Robin respected old Mr. Smith so much. And not only because he was a war veteran who had lost part of a foot fighting in Vietnam. He was also smart, kind, and a true friend. Without Mr. Smith, Robin in da hood would never have happened.

"I'm sorry, Mr. Smith. I really wanted to get those candlesticks for Missus Collins," Robin murmured.

Mr. Smith gazed at Robin and then toward the front door of the Shrimp Shack. Robin followed his eyes. Missus Collins had just presented the candlesticks to her daughter Denise. Denise was a well-dressed woman of almost fifty who looked very much like her mother. Robin had heard that while Missus Collins had never finished junior high, Denise was a lawyer. The two of them looked so happy.

*That scene? That scene wouldn't be happening if we hadn't gone back for those sticks. That's true for sure. It's also true I could have died. My friends could have died too. Was it worth it? Would I do it again if I knew everything that would happen? That the bank of badness would*

*be shut down? That the Rangers would be*
*shooting at us?*

Robin was honest with himself.

*I'm not sure.*

"You say you got outta there without
sayin' anyone's name?" Mr. Smith's voice
got Robin's attention again.

Robin nodded.

"And you told Kaykay's folks she had
an allergic reaction? An' they bought what
you was sellin'?"

Robin nodded again.

"And you went back there because
Missus Collins was so kind to Dorothy—
ahem, Miz Paige?"

Robin startled, even as he nodded one
more time. Mr. Smith had just referred to his
grandmother by her first name. Dorothy. No
one called her that. Even her closest friends
called her Miz Paige.

Except for Mr. Smith.

*Man, I gotta talk to my gramma.*

"Everything okay?" Sly stopped working for a second to check in. Robin was glad for the company.

"Fine, fine," Mr. Smith said.

"That's good!" Kaykay popped up on the other side of the counter and leaned into the conversation.

"You been listening?" Robin asked her.

"Listenin' to what?" Kaykay acted all innocent. Then she winked at Robin. He grinned back at her. He'd wanted her to hear his conversation with Mr. Smith. Evidently, she just had. That was so Kaykay.

"I think you kids need to listen up," Mr. Smith said, though he faced Robin. His voice was gentle. Comforting.

*How a grandpa might talk to a grandkid,* Robin thought.

"Robin told me everything. I was mad, at first. But then again, when I was fourteen, I woulda done the same thing," Mr. Smith chuckled. "Only difference is, I woulda got myself shot. No regrets, Robin. Okay?"

Robin thought those were nice words that didn't have much juice. He had so many regrets.

"We should have called you first," Robin shared.

Mr. Smith smiled broadly. "Like I said, when I was fourteen, I woulda done the same as you. So, who wants to bring me some of that fine cake?"

Kaykay raised her hand. "I'll do it. But you gotta maybe help me with something first."

She sketched out the Tyrone situation at school and asked Mr. Smith if he had any ideas.

Mr. Smith shook his head. "Gotta think on that one, Kaykay."

"The dude's a pig. An' a gangsta! An' a drug dealer!" she exclaimed. "He all in my business. It's disgustin', and I'm over it. We need to shut him down."

*Drug dealer. That's it.*

Robin punched the air. "I got it!"

"Got what?" Sly asked.

"Got how to nail Tyrone and get Kaykay back to us. Now listen up."

# Chapter Five

On Monday, Robin and Sly had to deal yet again with the sights and sounds of Team Tyrone at Ironwood Central High School. This time, Tyrone's arm had been draped over Kaykay's shoulder as they came into the cafeteria for lunch. Her arm was around Tyrone's waist.

It made Robin want to puke up his mystery meat.

She didn't look at Robin. He didn't look at her. It was how they'd planned it. They wanted Tyrone to think that Kaykay was now ready to take it to the next level.

That had been the setup. Now, after school, it was time for the payoff.

As he and his buds walked along Randolph Road—a street of nasty walk-up apartment buildings that ran parallel to Garvey—they went over their plan.

"The shades work?" Robin asked Kaykay.

Kaykay nodded. "I checked 'em out in the bathroom at school. They work great."

"Batteries still good?" Sly queried.

Kaykay nodded again. "Far as I know."

Robin was satisfied. When he and his friends had bought a bunch of spy gear before their first operation at the bank of badness, they'd picked up some sunglasses that had a tiny built-in movie camera. When the camera was turned on, it filmed whatever the wearer was seeing. Robin didn't know then what they could be useful for but thought it would be good to have them in their arsenal. Today, Kaykay was going to put said glasses to use.

"Okay. Put 'em on," Robin instructed. "I want to see how they look."

Kaykay found the shades in her backpack. They were nothing special to look at. If a person didn't know in advance that they hid a 1.8-megapixel camera and an eight-gig memory card, no one would suspect a thing.

*That's the whole idea*, Robin thought as they neared Twenty-Eighth Street. *If this works …*

Robin tried not to get his hopes up, but they got up anyway. If his plan worked, Tyrone and Dodo would be out of his life for a long time, which meant that Kaykay could start being friends with him and Sly in public again. That would be a dream come true. He missed not being able to hang with her at school, and he hated seeing her with Tyrone. Deep down, he was afraid that Tyrone might put her in a position that she couldn't get out of, so to speak. Kaykay was a fast-talker with a big mouth, but Robin thought that if things went even a couple more days with Tyrone, Kaykay might find herself in a sitch where talk would be useless.

As the three kids reached the corner of Twenty-Eighth and Randolph, they stopped.

"We split up here," Robin told them. "Kaykay, good luck."

"I'm gonna kill it," Kaykay said confidently. "Just wait and see."

"Give us three minutes to get in position," Robin reminded her. "Then do your thing."

There were a few hugs. Then Robin and Sly crossed the street and went into the first apartment building on the corner. They'd done a dry run after Missus Collins's party. They knew they could climb the stairs of this building and come out on the roof. Then, jumping rooftop to rooftop, they'd work their way to the corner of Twenty-Eighth Street and Garvey, where they'd have a sixth-story bird's-eye view on what was happening on the street below.

Everything worked perfectly. Three minutes after they got into the first building, Robin and Sly were leaning over the parapet wall of the apartment building closest to the corner of Garvey. They were super careful. A fall meant death. But from here, they could take in one of the roughest corners in the hood, where the Ninth Street Rangers did a lot of drug dealing. Tyrone and his homeboy Dodo often worked this corner for the Rangers.

Robin peered down, looking for his two enemies. He didn't see them.

"Bogeys at nine o'clock!" Sly pointed.

"What?"

"Bogeys at nine o'clock. That means, enemy planes coming from the left," Sly explained as he pointed to Tyrone and Dodo. "It's what they say in the movies."

"Get serious, dude." Robin spotted Tyrone and Dodo. They had the black bandanas of the Ninth Street Rangers slung through the belt loops of their shorts.

Where was Kaykay?

*Ah!* There she was, on the same side of the street as Tyrone. As planned, she stopped and hung out about fifty yards from Tyrone and Dodo, waiting for a car to pull up near them.

It didn't take long. Within a minute or two, a cream-colored Lexus with a couple of kids in the front seat slowed to a stop. Robin saw Tyrone approach the driver. Meanwhile, Kaykay approached Tyrone. Even though he was making the deal, Tyrone took a moment to embrace her.

Then Kaykay stood close as the dude in the Lexus handed Tyrone some cash. Tyrone took a little glassine bag from Dodo and passed it to the driver. There was a fist bump between Tyrone and the driver—clearly, this wasn't their first deal—and then the car roared off.

*Probably headin' back to the Richie burbs*, Robin figured. *Those kids come to our hood to buy their crack or 420, then go home to use. Meanwhile, gangbangers are blowing each other away for the chance to sell to them.*

*There's somethin' wrong with that.*

"Okay, now for the hard part," Sly told him.

"I know," Robin muttered.

There was one more part of the plan for Kaykay to execute. They wanted Tyrone to think that Kaykay had come by because she missed him so much that she just had to see him. There was only one way to do that. ...

"Here it come," Sly announced.

Robin forced himself to watch, just in case there was a problem. If there was, he and Sly planned to yell for help and call 911. Both boys held their breath.

Kaykay kissed Tyrone. Big time.

"Mission accomplished," Sly told Robin.

Robin winced. "Yeah. I guess. Let's get out of here."

---

"What do I do with this damn thing?" Mr. Smith asked as he fingered the memory card from Kaykay's sunglasses.

"You push it in the slot in the computer," Sly instructed.

"You do it, Robin." Mr. Smith passed the little card to Robin. "I can pick a lock, but I don't know nothing about computers."

It was a half hour later. After Kaykay had kissed Tyrone—Robin still couldn't get the picture of that out of his mind—they'd all met up at Twenty-Seventh and Randolph.

Then they'd practically run to the Center on Garvey near Ninth Street.

They were so pumped to see what Kaykay had recorded. Robin was nervous. What if the tech had failed? Had they taken the risk for nothing? Even worse, had Kaykay just kissed Tyrone for nothing?

They were with Mr. Smith in the Center's small library. That library—not really more than a room with a few bookshelves, desks, and chairs—had one computer that wasn't even connected to the Internet. But it would be fine for what they needed to do: see what Kaykay's sunglasses had captured.

Mr. Smith closed and locked the door. They would only need a few minutes.

Robin took the memory card from Mr. Smith, sat at the computer, and popped the card into the right slot. Almost immediately, the computer read the card and opened a folder. It took Robin a little while longer to find the right video player. When he did, he pressed the Play arrow.

"Oh my God," Kaykay whispered. "It worked."

The sunglasses video camera had recorded everything. It was a little herky-jerky, but the four of them watched a two-minute video of Tyrone taking the money, getting the glassine bag from Dodo, and handing it to the kids in the car.

Robin stopped the video right there. They had enough to send Tyrone and Dodo to juvie for long time. No reason to watch the rest. No reason to endure that kiss again. Too painful.

"Okay. We got what we need. Now how do we nail Tyrone and Dodo? If they find out that Kaykay filmed them, we're dead," Sly observed.

Robin had a solution he thought would be foolproof.

"We don't bring it to the cops," he explained. "Instead, Mr. Smith takes it to Principal Kwon. He doesn't even give it to him. He just shows it to him. Says that these dudes need to be outta Ironwood Central. We let Principal Kwon take it from there."

Mr. Smith nodded. "Smart, Robin Paige. Very smart. I'll do that in the morning."

"What if Mr. Kwon asks Mr. Smith where he got it?" Kaykay asked.

"I just gave him fifty thou for his school library. He won't ask. An' if he does, I'll just say I got my ways," Mr. Smith told them.

Robin shut down the computer, popped out the memory card, and gave it to Mr. Smith. "Thanks. Now can you and Sly go set up to play cards? I need to talk to Kaykay for a sec. We'll be right out."

There was no argument. Robin was their leader, even if there was no more Robin in da hood. Twenty seconds later, Robin and Kaykay were alone.

"So," Robin said to her. "I just wanted to say good job."

"I did good?"

Robin nodded.

"Was it all good, Robin?" Kaykay asked softly.

Robin hesitated and then shook his head. "Nope. It wasn't all good."

"What wasn't all good, Robin?"

He felt hot blood rush to his cheeks. "Day-um, Kaykay. You oughta know what part. I hated the part where you kiss—"

He never finished his sentence. Kaykay's lips were on his. She kissed him. He kissed her back. The longer the kiss went, the further the memory of Kaykay's staged lip-lock with Tyrone slid out of his mind.

It didn't take long for it to be all gone.

# Chapter Six

Tuesday morning, Robin walked to school the usual way. Ninth Street was quiet at seven forty-five. There was a bit of a chill in the air that promised autumn was coming, though the few scraggly trees in planters on the sidewalk hadn't yet turned color. Robin liked this time of year and this time of day. It was peaceful. Ninth Street had been quiet for the last couple of weeks in general. No fights, no shootings, no arrests.

Robin knew what that meant. Calm before the storm. What the storm would be was anyone's guess. He just hoped that he and his grandmother would not be involved.

At the corner of Ninth and Garvey, he turned left. Then he noticed that new business again. The garage door was open, and a gorgeous sports car was being driven inside. This time it was a red Lamborghini coming in for repairs. *Wow.* Robin was impressed.

He checked his cell. He had plenty of time. He decided to go around the back, to the alley behind the shop. He thought maybe there'd be some cool cars there to check out—cars that had already been worked on. He wasn't all that into cars, to tell the truth, but Sly was crazed for them. Maybe he could bring Sly back here to check them out.

*Sly's crazed for anything that costs lots of chip because it means you gotta have the chip in the first place*, Robin thought with a smile.

It was a quick walk to the alley and a quicker walk to the back of the business.

Robin expected to see a bunch of gorgeous cars parked there, all fixed up and waiting for their owners.

There was nothing. In fact, there wasn't even a rear garage door. Just a plain old door with a latch handle.

*Huh. Very strange.*

Above the door was a small window. Robin told himself that sometime he needed to take a look through that window. Cars were coming into this business, but none were coming out.

It didn't make any sense at all.

Robin was sitting at free breakfast with Sly—Kaykay was with Tyrone and Dodo at the next table—when it happened.

Four uniformed Ironwood Police Department officers marched into the cafeteria. Two were black, one was Latino, and one was white. They were all big and intimidating. As Robin and his buds watched, the cops marched straight over to the table where Tyrone and Dodo were holding forth. Robin saw that Kaykay was fake-laughing up a storm.

Cops in the lunchroom were a big deal. All talk stopped, except for Tyrone. He hadn't noticed the police.

"So I was tellin' my boy Dodo here—"

"Tyrone Davis? Riondo Moore?" The biggest and most imposing of the policemen shouted Tyrone and Dodo's names.

Finally, Tyrone quit talking. The cafeteria was so quiet Robin could hear the air conditioner humming.

"Yessir," he said to the cop. "I'm Tyrone Davis."

"An' I'm Riondo Moore," Dodo added.

It was funny for Robin to see how polite the junior Rangers were being. He had an idea what this was about. If he was right …

The four cops moved in, two on each side of each guy.

"You're both under arrest!" the lead cop declared. "You have the right to remain silent. Everything you say can and will be used against you in a court of law. You have the right to an attorney. If you cannot afford an attorney, one will be provided for you. Do you understand these rights?"

The cops jerked Tyrone and Dodo to their feet and cuffed them as everyone stared. Robin figured half of the people at free breakfast were cheering inside because they hated Tyrone and Dodo as much as Robin did. The other half would have jumped the cops—if the cops hadn't been packing—because they distrusted the police on principle.

"Yeah, I understand!" Tyrone said loudly, full of bravado. "Whatchu arrestin' us for?"

"For being an idiot!" one of the black cops told him. "You got drugs in your school locker to sell. So does your boy Dodo. Now, you're comin' with us!"

The moment they were all out of the door, the cafeteria erupted in conversations, shouting, and pointing. This was big news. Kaykay ran right over to Robin and Sly. "Mr. Smith did it! He did it! He did it! Them gangstas are outta my life. Gone, gone, gone!"

So excited, she hugged Sly and Robin. Robin flushed. Sly just looked sad. Robin realized that Sly knew about his and Kaykay's mini-romance and wished it was him instead of Robin.

*We gotta get Sly a fly girl*, Robin thought.

Just then, as if by magic, a fly girl approached them. The only problem was it wasn't the fly girl Robin was hoping for. In fact, it was the worst possible fly girl.

Her name was Chantelle Price. Chantelle was a tenth grader who wrote a gossip column for the school paper. She had a rep for digging up dirt and sharing it in her column; sometimes she even posted it online or Tweeted it. Robin had never met her, but he already knew who she was by her rep.

Chantelle was hot. Tall, legs up to there and curves in all the right places, with a great sense of style. She managed to rock her school uniform blue skirt and blue top by adding dangling earrings and a blue necklace.

*Uh-oh.* Robin noticed she was carrying the little notebook she used whenever she was working on a story.

"Hey, kids!" Chantelle plopped down next to them. "I'm Chantelle and I write for the school paper. Mind if I ask a couple of questions?"

"Fine with us," Robin muttered. He hoped it had nothing to do with Robin in da hood. He knew that refusing could turn into a story itself and would only get Chantelle more interested.

Chantelle turned to Kaykay. "That was your man bein' taken away, right?"

"I was hangin' wit' him, but I wouldn't 'zactly call him 'my man,' " Kaykay answered.

"That's not what I would say," Chantelle fired back.

"Then you buggin' and makin' things up in your mind," Kaykay responded.

Chantelle smiled and jotted a few words in her notebook. "Really. I just think it's interesting that your man got arrested 'bout a nanosecond ago, and now you're back with your old friends. What's up with that?"

Kaykay looked caught. Robin kicked himself. He knew they should have given it a little time before they started hanging together. A week. Even a day. Chantelle was right. This was suspicious.

Chantelle leaned in toward Kaykay. "You wanna know what I'm thinking, Karen?" She called Kaykay by her real name, not by her nickname. "I'm thinking maybe you were the one who turned your man in. Know what we call that 'round here? We call that snitchin'. And peeps 'round this school don't like that none."

Robin thumped the table with his hand. "Kaykay is not a snitch!"

Chantelle smiled. "Really? Why don't you prove it?"

The bell rang. Time for class. Kaykay took the opportunity to hustle away. Robin knew they'd been saved for the moment, but that the bell couldn't save them forever. One problem was gone, but another had taken its place. Her name was Chantelle.

# Chapter Seven

Robin Paige! What a surprise!"

Robin was walking down Garvey toward Ninth Street when he heard his name called from behind him. He turned. *Oh no.* It was Chantelle Price again, this time not fifteen feet away.

*How long has she been following me? Has she been on my tail all the way home from school?*

It was the same day that Tyrone and Dodo were arrested. The school had been buzzing with the news. During lunch, Robin had received a call from Mr. Smith. Everything had gone perfectly with the principal. He'd shown Principal Kwon the video Kaykay had shot. The principal didn't even ask who'd taken it; he just called the police and asked them to search Tyrone and Dodo's lockers. The cops had found crack, crank, and 420 in each dude's locker. That had led to the arrests. There was no question that the boys would be headed for juvie until they turned eighteen.

Robin stopped and turned back. "Hey, Chantelle. Whatchu doin' in this hood? You live 'round here?" He made his voice "street" to make himself sound tougher.

Chantelle laughed. "Why you be talkin' like a gangsta when you got a four-oh average like me?"

" 'Cause you not answerin' my question," Robin replied. "That be why."

"Good answer," Chantelle acknowledged.

Both Robin and Chantelle smiled, but Robin was still wary of the tenth grader.

He didn't want him or his friends to be the subject of any of her gossipy stories. That might make other people start to compare notes, which would not be good. All they needed was for the Rangers to learn that he'd ripped them off a couple of times. …

"Where's your friend Kaykay? And your ace, Sly?" Chantelle asked.

Robin shrugged. "Don't know. You'll have to find them yourself."

Chantelle flipped her long dark hair. She was a good seven inches taller than Robin. "Maybe I will. I got some good news for them."

"Oh?"

She waited for a dump truck to roar by on Garvey before she continued. "Mmm-hmm. Turns out Kaykay didn't snitch. I heard the crazy old man who gave the money to the library last week blew the whistle."

"Mr. Smith isn't crazy," Robin said quickly, then instantly regretted his words. There was no reason for Chantelle to know anything more about Mr. Smith.

Chantelle jumped on this immediately. "You know him? How do you know him? Does Sly know him too?"

Robin wasn't sure what to say, and he sure couldn't figure out Chantelle's new interest in Sly. Hadn't she been focused on Kaykay? He did some quick thinking. Now that Chantelle knew Mr. Smith's name, it wouldn't be hard to track him down. She'd probably ask him a bunch of questions. If he tried to evade her, she'd just talk to people who knew him at the Center.

*Better for me to tell her and manage the four-one-one.*

"Yeah, we all know him," Robin admitted. "From the community center."

"Is he your friend? Is he Sly's friend?"

"You could say that," Robin allowed.

"Who's a better friend of his, you or Sly?"

*Enough*, Robin thought. *What am I, Wikipedia?*

"I gotta get home and do my home-work," Robin mumbled. "Then I gotta help my gramma."

Chantelle nodded. "Okay. Then we're done for now. Emphasis on now. I'm glad Kaykay isn't a snitch, by the way. The Rangers wouldn't like that." Then she frowned. "But I still can't figure out why she sat down with you and Sly right after Tyrone and Dodo got cuffed. Doesn't make sense."

"We live in Ironwood," Robin told her. "A lotta stuff 'round here doesn't make sense. See ya."

He turned and started down Garvey again. At the corner of Ninth Street, he glanced over his shoulder. Chantelle was still watching him. She gave him a little wave, then stepped away in the opposite direction.

*Huh. Strange. Why is she so interested in us all of a sudden? And what's with all these questions about Sly?*

Robin found himself across the street from the new auto repair shop. Rather than go straight home to his apartment, he decided to watch the place for a while. He edged into the doorway of a vacant storefront and waited. And waited. And waited some more.

Nothing. It was like no one was there.

Just before he gave up, he took a few mental notes. First, the address: 919 Marcus Garvey Boulevard. He got a good look at the front door. It had three locks on it. No signage at all. Nothing to indicate the name of the business, its hours, or the type of business it was. In fact, Robin noticed that the garage door had been replaced. The new one looked heavier and sturdier. It looked strong enough to hold off a battering ram.

*Those people sure don't want anyone coming in*, Robin thought. *Okay. Time to go home.*

As he stepped out of the doorway, though, action started. He turned to observe from a safe distance. First, the garage door went up. Then, a couple of guys came outside. They were in their twenties or thirties, wearing identical blue mechanics' coveralls. Ten seconds later, an older red Honda Accord pulled up to the driveway. A forty-something Latino guy drove it. The guys waved the car inside, stepped into the building, and then slid the door down with a clang that Robin could hear down the street.

Robin waited for the driver to come out. But the driver never came out.

*All right. This is weird. I gotta find out what's going on in there.*

Robin ran home, passing the Rangers' drug dealers doing their thing. He said a quick hello to his grandmother down in the Shrimp Shack, then hurried up to his room and booted up his computer. He wanted to research the business, but he didn't have much to go on. He checked the address against official Ironwood business records to see if he could find the name of the owner and the kind of work they did.

Nothing.

He checked a couple of other databases, like the crisscross directory that listed telephone numbers by addresses. More nothing. It was like the new business on the corner didn't exist. Then he got a brainstorm. Who owned the building? If he could find out who owned the building, he could call the owner and ask what was up.

Robin went into the city real estate records. Bingo. There was an owner listed for the building at 919 Marcus Garvey Boulevard. The only problem, Robin saw it was a Delaware corporation called Acme Corporation. And when he looked up Acme Corporation in Delaware, he saw that it was a sub-group of a different corporation.

He banged his fists on the desk in frustration. This wasn't getting anywhere.

He was about to start his homework when he decided to look up one more thing. Before the disaster at the U-Store, Robin had planted a GPS tracking device in one of the Rangers' cars. That GPS device had led them right to the bank of badness at the U-Store. He wondered if it was still working.

It only took a second to switch over to the GPS program and a moment later for the familiar red dot to show up on the screen. That was good. The GPS was working. The only problem? The Rangers' car was no longer in Ironwood. Robin found himself looking at a map of Dallas, Texas.

*They must have sold the car. Or gotten it out of town.*

Whichever one it was, Robin knew that the GPS was now useless. He'd hoped against hope that it might lead him to a new bank of badness. No such luck.

He turned off the computer, lay down on his bed fully dressed, and closed his eyes for a moment. He didn't intend to nap, but he did.

He dreamed that the Rangers were after him again. So were the guys who worked at the business at the corner of Garvey and Ninth. So was the Ironwood Police Department. And so was Chantelle Price.

It was a nightmare.

# Chapter Eight

It was three days later. Robin was down in the Shrimp Shack getting ready to take the usual Friday protection money to the Rangers. They always paid a hundred a week, though the Rangers had talked about a price increase. After his experience at the U-Store, Robin wasn't sure that paying off the Rangers was such a bad idea. Better than getting gunned down by them or having the Shrimp Shack torched.

"You don't have to take the money to the Rangers for another twenty minutes, Robin," his grandmother said. "Have some fine shrimp."

"Okay, Gramma," Robin said. "I will."

He never tired of his grandmother's fried shrimp, which was a good thing since he had it for dinner three or four times a week. His friend Kaykay, who was vegan, winced every time Robin told her he'd had shrimp for dinner. She went on and on about how Robin was ruining his arteries.

Robin chewed a couple of shrimp and washed them down with some lemonade his grandmother had poured for him. She was a big woman, as tall as many men and hefty in a white chef's outfit. She nodded approvingly as he ate. She was okay for someone who had recently been gravely ill.

"Can I ask you something, Gramma?"

"You keep eatin' yo' shrimp like that, you can ask me anything," Miz Paige responded.

"How come you never told me you knew Mr. Smith?"

Robin had been waiting for the right opportunity to talk to his grandmother about Mr. Smith. Now was the time. He'd asked it point blank. He saw his grandmother stiffen. A little vein above her left eye throbbed.

*Why is she reacting like this?*

"Well …" His grandmother seemed to be choosing her words with care. "You never asked me."

It was almost exactly the same thing that Mr. Smith had told him.

*What a dodge!*

"That's not saying much," Robin commented.

"Keep eatin' yo' shrimp," Miz Paige instructed. "You a growin' boy."

"That's not saying much," Robin repeated. But he took another shrimp anyway.

"Then I'll say mo', though this brings back some memories I don't want to remember, necessarily. Mr. Smith and your late

79

grandfather Horace and me were all good friends back before your father was born," Miz Paige shared. "After your father came along, we sort of stopped bein' such good friends."

"Really?" Robin was fascinated. "How come?"

"He and Horace had a fallin' out over something. Horace never told me. I never asked. It don't matter none now. Maybe Mr. Smith will tell you more. Maybe—"

She stopped talking. Her eyes swung to the door. So did Robin's.

Two Ninth Street Rangers had just stepped into the shop. One of them was the guy with the shaved head and mole under his nose, who was in the car when Robin did his usual payoffs. The other guy was new. Almost as tall as the leader, with long sideburns and wild eyes. Both gangstas wore all black, with black bandanas tied through their belt loops.

"We want to talk to Shrimp," the leader announced from the doorway.

Miz Paige bristled. "His name is Robin. This is my shop. If you've come for my hard-earned money, I'll give it to you. Just remember that when you're in my shop, you talk to me."

The leader smiled, flashing a new gold tooth.

"We want to talk to Robin," he intoned, using Robin's real name instead of his hated nickname. "You stand outside while we talk. You can watch through the glass. But this is between him and us. We gonna talk a little bid'ness with Robin."

"No!" Miz Paige refused.

The leader turned to her. "Miz Paige? If you know what's good for you, you *will* step outside the door."

Robin's heart thumped. He felt a bead of sweat roll down his back. Were the Rangers here to talk to him about what happened at the U-Store? Had they figured out that it was him and his friends? If they had, what were they going to do?

He clutched the table. *Maybe they want to kill me in front of my gramma.*

There was nothing he could do except wait for it to happen. Meanwhile, his grandmother moved toward the door. With one last look at Robin, she stepped outside. A moment later, Robin could see her nose pressed against the glass door.

The two Rangers pulled up chairs and sat in them backward, facing Robin. Robin waited for them to pull out their Glocks and waste him. The only thing that kept him from crying out and running was his fear that they'd gun down his grandmother after they did him. If he kept calm, maybe he could save her life.

They didn't shoot him. But what they said shot him through his soul.

First, the leader introduced himself.

"Robin, you can call me Master. Everybody else do that. My boy here, you don't gotta know his name. Not yet, anyway. Whatchu wan' us to call you?"

"Robin," he croaked.

"Okay, Robin it be, no mo' Shrimp," Master promised.

"Why you wan' talk to me?" Robin asked them.

Master and his sidekick exchanged a smile.

"Speak good English," Master told Robin. "That's why we want to talk to you. Don't be someone you ain't. Recently, there was a problem at your school," Master went on. "Two of our junior boys got themselves popped. They had drugs in their lockers.

They gonna be in juvie till they turn eigh-teen. Maybe longer. Stupid be as stupid do, you know what I'm sayin'?"

Robin thought the smart thing to do was nod, though he didn't know what Master was saying at all. Or at least, not where the Rangers' boss was heading with this.

"We been doin' some talkin', and we been thinkin' we need some junior Rangers who gots brains, Robin. Some that be smart enough not to take drugs to school. Smart enough not to talk 'bout what they doin' as Rangers. Smart enough to speak good English to the po-lice. Smart enough that peeps won't think they be Rangers. Know what I'm sayin'?"

Robin nodded again, though a pit big enough for his heart to fall through had wid-ened in his belly. If this was going where he thought it was going. …

Master leaned forward so that the chair he was on tilted on two legs. "I want you—and maybe your two friends, Kaykay and Sly—don't ask me how I know 'bout 'em, I know everythin' 'bout everythin'—to think 'bout becomin' Rangers."

*Oh my God. He wants me and my friends in his gang!*

"We'll talk mo' 'bout this next week," Master told Robin. "Jus' wanted you to start to think on it. Could be real good for you. Okay to talk wit' your homeboy and homegirl 'bout this. Not your grandma. We out now."

He and the other Ranger headed for the door. As they did, Robin realized they hadn't asked for their usual protection money.

The moment they were gone, Miz Paige rushed over to Robin. "What did they want from you?"

Robin's head was spinning. No way was he gonna do what Master asked him.

"They want me and my friends to join their gang."

"No!" Miz Paige thundered. "No, no, no!"

Robin was about to say more, when he saw someone looking through the glass door of the Shrimp Shack.

Not Master or his scary homeboy.

Chantelle Price.

"Hey!" he shouted. "What do you want? What do you want?!"

By the time he ran to the door, she was gone.

# Chapter Nine

Early Saturday morning, Robin went with his grandmother to one of her endless doctors' appointments at the community clinic. The doctors wanted to do a follow-up on her Lyme disease treatment and some other blood tests. Miz Paige took a fistful of pills a few times a day for achy joints, diabetes, and high cholesterol. It scared Robin a lot.

*If she dies, I'm all alone.*

As usual, the clinic was jammed. The waiting room had benches instead of chairs, and every inch was taken up with poor folks of all ages, sizes, and shapes. There were plenty of screaming babies too. It made

Robin think that if any place in the hood needed a big donation of money, this was it. More doctors, more nurses, and a better waiting room.

A million dollars could do the trick, he figured.

He winced. He might have had access to that kind of money at the bank of badness, once upon a time. The thought made Robin mad at himself all over again.

At ten o'clock, Miz Paige insisted that Robin head over to the Center. Saturday mornings there were special; the young members made and served a hot breakfast to the old people. The meal wasn't fancy— sometimes it was just reheated fast food egg sandwiches or hotcakes. But since many of the old folks were living on Social Security, free food was a big deal.

By ten thirty, Robin was in a white apron behind a buffet table, with Kaykay to his left and Sly to his right. They were all supposed to be helping the old folks with their food, but only Robin and Kaykay were actually serving. Sly was doing magic tricks.

"Step right up and pick a card," Sly told an old lady named Wanda. "Any card!"

"Let Wanda eat her breakfast before you do the morning entertainment," Kaykay growled. Then she turned to Wanda. "Can I help you with your tray, Wanda?"

"That would be lovely, Kaykay," Wanda said. Then she winked at Sly. "Maybe you can give me a private magic show sometime, you handsome boy."

Kaykay hooted. "Wanda, are you flirtin' with Sly?"

"He a handsome boy; he deserve some flirtin'," Wanda said. Kaykay prepared Wanda's tray with a plate of hotcakes, fresh fruit, and a cup of hot coffee. She escorted Wanda to her table and gently set down her tray.

When Kaykay was gone, Sly lamented, "Only girl interested in me is a hundred zillion years old!"

"That is not true," Robin told him as he loaded plates for the other diners.

"Well, Kaykay be all into you. Tell who be all into me?" Sly went on.

Robin didn't really have an answer for him. "Wanda said you're handsome," he deflected, mock-punching Sly's arm.

"Handsome? No way, no how!" Sly was aghast. "Handsome? I'm funny. I'm talented. I'm a good person. But I'm as big as a house."

"Lotta girls don't care about that," Robin assured him. He poured out five cups of coffee and put them where the senior citizens could easily reach them.

"Oh yeah? Like who?" Sly challenged.

Robin pursed his lips. He knew he was in no position to give girl advice to his buddy. Kaykay was his first girlfriend. At least, he thought she was his girlfriend, even though they'd never gone on an actual date.

*Does that mean I need to ask her out? To the movies or something? If I do, how am I gonna pay for it? I don't even get an allowance!*

Money was still on his mind when he and his friends sat down to eat with Mr. Smith. Robin, Mr. Smith, and Sly all had hotcakes, bananas, and buttered biscuits. Kaykay the vegan had brought a salad of bean sprouts and organic tomatoes.

"Maybe I should be eating that," Sly said, looking at the salad dubiously. "Could help me drop three or four of my spare tires. Of course, that'd leave six or seven to go."

"Can we talk about something else, please?" Robin suggested. "A couple of Rangers came to the Shrimp Shack."

Mr. Smith swallowed a bite of his biscuit. "To pick up their payoff, no doubt."

Robin shook his head. "Nope. They didn't take any money. Instead they asked me—and maybe Sly and Kaykay too—to join up with their gang. Said they needed some brains. Not knuckleheads like Tyrone and Dodo."

"I ain't gonna be a Ranger!" Sly exclaimed. "No way, no how!"

"Tyrone be worse than a knucklehead. He be walking dog doo." Kaykay speared a tomato and forked it into her mouth.

"What'd you tell them?" Mr. Smith asked.

"I didn't tell them anything. They didn't want an answer. They just told me to think about it. But they wouldn't take any money. Didn't even ask for it."

Sly whistled. "I guess that means they be serious."

"What do we do?" Kaykay addressed the question not to everyone, but to Robin.

"Well, we sure aren't gonna say yes!" Robin responded.

"But you don't want to make them brothers mad, either," Mr. Smith advised them. He sipped his coffee. "A mad Ranger is a bad Ranger."

"I think it's good they're askin'," Kaykay told Robin. "It means they don't suspect you—us—all of us—of nothing else."

"So what I gotta do is figure out a way to say no, but not make them mad at us." Robin forked up the last bite of his hotcakes.

"What I wish is that we could still get into that storage room," Sly said softly. "I'd love to be the one to give my daddy the money for his mission."

Sly's words silenced the table. Robin still felt awful. It would have been so easy to get enough money from the bank of badness to send three church busses to the hurricane zone. They could have taken enough money to send thirty busses!

*And the community clinic? We coulda built them a whole new building.*

"I wish we could do that for you, Sly," Kaykay said honestly. "But that's just not how things worked out. We saved the Center, we saved the school library—sometimes you gotta be satisfied with what it is, not what it might be."

"I know we can't take mo' money from the Rangers," Sly agreed with her. "If only there was someone else bad we could hit up."

"There ain't no one," Mr. Smith said. "So let's finish up our breakfast and play some cards."

"No, Mr. Smith," Robin said suddenly.

"No what, Robin Paige? You don't want to play no cards? Whatchu want to do, then?" Mr. Smith asked.

Robin rubbed his chin. He did that a lot when he was thinking hard. "I'm thinkin' about what Sly just said." He stood. "Who's comin' with me?"

A half hour later, the four of them were standing on the opposite side of Garvey at Ninth Street, about a half block from the weird auto repair business.

Robin pointed to it. "That's the place."

"What about it?" Sly squinted in the midday sunshine. "It look normal."

"That's what I thought too, at first," Robin told him. "But I don't think that now. Now what I think we should do is walk down Garvey one at a time so no one gets suspicious—Kaykay, you walk with me, it's safer—and case the place. We'll meet at Garvey and Eighth. Mr. Smith, you go first."

The kids hid out of sight while Mr. Smith took his walk. Three minutes later,

Sly followed. And then Robin and Kaykay three minutes after that. Robin saw nothing out of the ordinary. Neither did Sly. However, when they met up again at Eighth and Garvey, out of sight of the strange business, Mr. Smith was agitated.

"Lemme tell you what I saw. As I was passin' the front, two dudes opened the garage. And then, like they'd timed it, another dude came flyin' in behind the wheel of an old Honda Civic. Then the first dudes pulled down the garage door like the sunshine was poison," Mr. Smith reported.

"I saw a Honda go in there too," Robin told them. "Last week. And no cars ever come out."

"Of course not," Mr. Smith declared. "Cars come in, but no cars go out. Except in parts, of course."

"I don't get it," Sly said.

"That's 'cause you a good human bein', Sly Thomas. Hondas are the most stolen car there is." Mr. Smith was all excited. "Ladies and gentlemen, Robin in da hood has uncovered a chop shop in da hood! Where they take cars and chop 'em up for their parts. Then they sell the parts to whoever wants them. Cheaper than buying from a factory."

Robin rubbed his chin again. "Well maybe … if it is what it seems to be—and that's a big if—maybe there's a way for us to make a withdrawal."

# Chapter Ten

Robin tightened his new black hoodie as he turned into the alley behind Ninth Street. He wore jeans and sneakers. In his pockets were his pepper spray and a flashlight. To his left was Sly, dressed the same way.

It was late Sunday afternoon. They were on their way to the chop shop—if that's what it was—to see if they could break in and maybe relieve the shop owners of some ill-gotten money. Kaykay couldn't be with them, since her parents were having relatives over for Sunday dinner, and she couldn't talk her way out of it. Mr. Smith, though, would be meeting them. Robin was counting on Mr. Smith's lock-picking skills to get them into the building.

*After that, it's up to Sly and me to find what we can find. Mr. Smith will stand guard outside.*

Robin was pretty confident there'd be no one inside. He and Sly had watched the front entrance for almost the entire afternoon, while Mr. Smith had been stationed at the alley. Two Latino guys left the shop at one thirty; neither had returned. The place was apparently deserted.

Of course, there was always the chance they'd surprise someone.

"You got your pepper spray?" Robin asked as they made their way along the alley.

Sly nodded. "You buggin', Robin. You asked before we left your grandma's place."

"Always worth a double check. Good thing she's volunteering at the church. We'd never be able to do this otherwise."

They got to the rear door of the chop shop and only had to wait a moment for Mr. Smith to hobble up to them. He wanted to go right to work on the lock, but Robin held him off.

"Boost me up to the window," he told Sly and Mr. Smith. "Lemme see if there's anything to see."

Mr. Smith and Sly agreed that this was a good idea. Robin put his right foot into Mr. Smith's linked fingers and his left foot into Sly's hands. Together, they lifted Robin so he had a good look into the shop.

*Crap*. The window now had a curtain over it. There was nothing—

"Hey! Hey! What are you doing there?"

Mr. Smith and Sly whirled; Robin lost his balance and fell clumsily to the ground. Someone had seen him. Was it one of the Latino guys? If it was, they were toast.

A moment later that someone came running up the alley. It wasn't a Latino guy. It wasn't a guy at all. It was Chantelle Price. She had on sneakers, shorts, and a red T-shirt. She was carrying her little reporter notebook.

*Oh no. This is bad. This is very, very bad.*

"Robin Paige! Sly Thomas! And you!" She pointed at Mr. Smith. "I know you. You're the guy who gave the money for our school library. What are you doing here?" She faced Sly. "Sly Thomas, if I didn't know any better, I'd say you were trying to break into this shop!"

Shy shook his head like it was attached to his neck by a loose spring. "No way, no how! We wouldn't do that! We were just … checkin' things out."

"That's right," Robin jumped in. "I saw that this business just opened, and it looked suspicious, so I wanted to maybe call the police."

"Like your friend Kaykay called the police on Tyrone and Dodo?" Chantelle smiled cockily.

"Kaykay didn't do anything," Mr. Smith told the girl. "I did. I was the one who went to the principal."

Chantelle made a face. "Tell me something I don't already know. What are you doing here, Sly?"

There was silence. Robin knew they were screwed.

"Nothing? No one has anything to say?"

More silence.

"Well then," Chantelle declared, "I have a proposition for you. Here it is. I think you're not helping the police. I think you're looking to see if there's money in there you can give away. I think you got the money to save the Center, and the money to save our library, and now you're looking for money for something else. You only take it from

bad people, and you give it to good people."
She gazed at Sly again. "Like your daddy
and his church. My cousin heard about your
church mission. Maybe you're looking for
money for that."

"What's your proposition?" Robin asked.
He tried to sound strong and confident.

"I'm going to write about all this in my
column," Chantelle told them. "Unless you
let me join you."

*What?*

Robin didn't answer her directly.
"Chantelle, you must be a good reporter if
you figured out what we've been doing."

Chantelle nodded. "It wasn't hard. I just
paid attention. Robin, for the last few days,
you've been watching this place. Everyone
at the Center says you and Sly and Mr.
Smith are like this. Kaykay too." She held
four fingers together. "Where there's smoke,
there's fire. Right now I think it's blazing."

"Then you don't want to get burned," Robin told her. "Smart thing for you to do is go on home and forget you were ever here. This is dangerous stuff."

Chantelle stood up to her full five foot eight. "Are you sayin' I can't handle myself?" She looked at Sly again. "I can handle myself just fine, Robin. Try me."

"Robin …" Mr. Smith pointed to his old-fashioned watch. Time was wasting. It was dangerous for them to be standing here yakking like this. No telling who might come along.

Robin made a quick decision that he realized he might regret. Big time.

"Okay, Chantelle," he declared. "You're in … if you promise to keep your mouth shut. No matter what!"

Chantelle nodded. "Thank you. I won't write about us, I won't Tweet about us, I won't speak about us. You can count on me."

Robin wasn't sure if that was true or not. Only time would tell.

"So we're going in there to see what we can see," Robin told her. "You, and me, and Sly. Mr. Smith, please give Chantelle your pepper spray."

Before he could, Chantelle displayed a small black container that was clipped to her keychain. "No need. I got my own. In this hood, a girl's gotta be prepared."

Robin nodded. "Good. Mr. Smith? Do your thing."

Mr. Smith took out a few of his old locksmithing tools and went to the rear door. "This is a lifter pin. What we've got here is an ordinary deadbolt. Should be a snap."

He slipped the lifter under the deadbolt lock and moved it gently, explaining that he was working the pins on the lock. Once the pins were up, he turned the door handle. The door opened easily.

"Close this behind us," Robin told Mr. Smith. "Knock if there's anything strange. Then run—well, walk fast. Come on, Sly. You too, Chantelle. We're going in."

Mr. Smith opened the door. Robin flicked on his flashlight and let his friends inside. There was a faint *click* as Mr. Smith closed the door behind them.

"Okay," Robin said. "Let's—"

He never got the words out. A snarling creature flew at them out of the darkness.

Robin had just enough time to swing his flashlight around. It was a German shepherd. A giant one. His mouth was open and his jaws dripped spittle as he leaped for Robin's throat!

# Chapter Eleven

In one motion, Robin pulled out his pepper spray and fired it at the German shepherd.

Direct hit. The attack dog yelped and seemed to change direction in midair. He fell heavily to the concrete floor and ran off in the other direction, mewling and howling.

"Follow that dog!" Robin ordered Sly and Chantelle. "Find some water and wash him off good. Especially his eyes. When you think you've done it enough, do it more. Be careful! Go on, do it!"

Sly and Chantelle ran off to find the dog. Robin shined his flashlight around the interior, looking for a light switch. He found it on the far wall, next to a tiny recessed office. He flicked it; the room was instantly bathed in harsh overhead light.

It took about two seconds of assessing for Robin to decide that Mr. Smith was absolutely right. There were stacks of car parts everywhere: tires, engines, bumpers, airbag consoles, windshields, doors, electronics, and more. Robin felt like he was in the middle of an auto parts store, except the parts were all stolen. The "business" was definitely a chop shop.

He had no idea how much all this was worth. Probably a lot. The question was, was there any money in this place that they could "withdraw" and give anonymously to the church for the mission? Robin figured they'd make the "withdrawal" and then call in a tip to the police in the morning. The cops would pay a visit, the guys running the chop shop would be arrested, and that would be that.

He went into the small office and started looking through drawers. Nothing. The drawers were empty. Same thing with the file cabinet.

"Any luck?"

Robin turned. It was Sly.

"How's the dog?" Robin asked.

"Better," Sly told him. "He's in some little back room. Chantelle's still washing out his eyes. You find anything?"

Robin shook his head. "Nah. Not yet. Help me look."

For the next five minutes, while Chantelle stayed with the dog, the two boys searched the shop. They came up empty. Either they weren't looking in the right place, or the crooks who ran the place didn't keep their cash there.

"You got anything?" Robin called to Sly, who was looking behind a rack of tools and blowtorches.

"Nope."

"Then we'd better get out of here." Robin cupped his hands and called toward the back. "Chantelle! How's the dog?"

"Okay!"

"Then let's roll!"

A moment later, Chantelle came out from the back room. Her shorts and half her T-shirt were soaked. "You said to use a lot of water," she told Robin.

"You're like, the attack dog whisperer," Sly commented, a wisecrack, which Chantelle found hysterically funny.

"You a funny boy," she told Sly.

"Let's discuss Sly's sense of humor somewhere else," Robin instructed. It wasn't likely that the crooks would return while they were in there, but he didn't want to take a chance. He'd already had that scary experience with the Rangers.

A minute later, the three of them were outside with Mr. Smith. They gave him the report: Yes, it's a chop shop. No, there's no cash.

"So whatchu want to do now?" Mr. Smith asked Robin.

"Let's call the cops," Robin decided. He looked at Sly. "You're the performer, make the call. Make it sound good."

Sly smiled. "I *so* have this covered."

Sly took out his cell and called the police. He reported that he had been walking in the alley near Ninth Street and Garvey and found the rear entrance to the business at 919 Garvey wide open. It looked like a chop shop. Not only that, there was a dog inside that looked hurt. Could the police come right away and maybe bring a vet too? In the meantime, he was going to call some friends to hang out till the police arrived.

Robin grinned when Sly was done. It was absolutely the perfect way to report what they'd found.

"You're a magician," Chantelle declared.

"You ain't seen nothin' yet," Sly promised her.

Sly's call was a big success. An Ironwood police cruiser pulled into the alley not ten minutes after Sly clicked off. Two cops got out. One was older and white, the other was younger and black. Robin recognized them immediately. They were Officer Leedham and Officer Goodall, the same cops who had barged into the Center a couple of weeks before to "arrest" Robin. In fact, they'd just wanted to talk with him and Miz Paige privately.

Mr. Smith and Sly recognized the cops too. "You two?" Sly exclaimed.

"We meet again," Leedham said, with a knowing look at Robin. "Who made the call?"

Sly raised his hand. "I did."

"Okay. Wait here while we take a look inside," Leedham instructed.

Guns in hand, the two cops entered the garage. Once the place was secure—Robin could have told them it was fine but knew he'd be better off saying nothing—Goodall called the city animal control department about the German shepherd. Leedham came back out to talk to the kids and Mr. Smith.

"Thank you, young man," he told Sly. "What's your name?"

"Sylvester Thomas. Call me Sly."

"Thank you, Sly. Your instincts are good. This is definitely a chop shop," Officer Leedham told him, then turned to the whole group. "My partner's gonna write up a report, and then you should all head home. We're gonna stake this place out and see if we can catch the perps. It could take a while. Maybe all night."

Officer Goodall took down everyone's name, address, and phone number. Then he asked Robin if he could talk with him privately.

"Sure, I guess," Robin said.

They walked together until they were out of earshot of the others.

"Your friend Sly? That's what Leedham and I were talking about with you and your grandmother," Goodall told Robin. "That's an example of what a good citizen does. Learn from him."

Robin nodded. No way could he tell the cop that he was the one responsible for blowing the whistle on this chop shop, not Sly. So he said the only thing he could.

"Okay, Officer Goodall. I will."

# Chapter Twelve

The next morning at free breakfast, Robin sat next to Kaykay, across from Chantelle and Sly. The breakfast, for a change, was something that Kaykay could actually eat— organic muffins made without eggs and cartons of soy milk instead of regular milk.

"You know why we're havin' this, don'chu?" Kaykay asked as she tore open the soy milk carton.

"Why do I have the feeling you're about to overshare?" Sly asked.

"Because I went to Principal Kwon, and I brought all kinds of articles about how soy milk is just as good as whole milk but even cheaper when you buy it in bulk," Kaykay said triumphantly. "And that some of us are vegan, which the school should do something about, didn't he think?"

Robin bit into the muffin. He wasn't going to say anything to Kaykay, but he thought it tasted like baked sawdust.

Chantelle tried the muffin too. "Omigod, Kaykay. This is unbelievable!"

"Unbelievable good or unbelievable bad?" Kaykay asked, with doubt in her voice.

"Unbelievable good! What else organic is this good?"

Sly groaned. "Oh no. Don't tell me that you both are going natural!"

Chantelle flipped her dark hair. "If I did, would you?"

"No!"

Chantelle flipped her hair again. "We'll see about that."

Everyone laughed. Robin felt great. True, they hadn't found any money they could donate to the church for the mission, but he, Sly, and Kaykay had made a new friend who was willing to help them with their operations. It made Robin think that maybe, just maybe, Robin in da hood could get back into business again.

*If we're careful*, he told himself.

"Kids? Can I have your attention, please?"

Robin heard a strange voice behind him. He turned. It was Principal Kwon's secretary. She was white, stout, and had a severely short hairdo. Robin didn't even know her name.

The conversation stopped.

"I'm Ms. Maxwell, Principal Kwon's administrative aide," she barked. "If you children are Robinson Paige, Sylvester Thomas, and Chantelle Price, please come with me. Principal Kwon wants to see you. Right now."

Robin worried as Ms. Maxwell led the way to Principal Kwon's private office. What could this possibly be about? Plus, it felt awful to leave Kaykay behind. But Ms. Maxwell made it clear that only Robin, Chantelle, and Sly were to follow her.

She showed them into Mr. Kwon's office. To Robin's surprise, Officers Leedham and Goodall from Ironwood PD were in there too. They stood near the bookcase while Mr. Kwon finished a phone call.

*This must have something to do with yesterday. But what? Have the cops figured out that we were inside the chop shop before they were? But Sly told them that he'd looked inside!*

Robin and his friends were ushered into three waiting chairs. Principal Kwon stood.

"Good to see you here. These policemen wanted to talk to you. Officer Leedham?"

The older cop took a few steps toward them. "I wanted to thank you all again in front of your principal," he said. "Especially Sly. Because of his actions and his quick thinking, we managed to break up an auto theft ring that has taken down more than two hundred vehicles in the last three months. The guys running it were career crooks."

Officer Goodall joined his partner. "It was big. So big that there was a major reward posted for the arrest of the ringleaders. We managed to pop them all last night, thanks to your help, Sly."

Major reward? Robin looked at his friend. Sly's jaw hung slack.

"Since they confessed, there's no doubt about a conviction," Leedham went on. "Sly, it could take a month or two, but the reward will be yours."

For a moment, there was silence in the room. Then Sly jumped to his feet and punched the air. "Yes! Yes, yes, yes!"

Everyone laughed, even Principal Kwon.

Sly was getting a reward. Robin thought it couldn't happen to a better buddy.

---

"Ten thousand dollars?" Mr. Smith exclaimed. "You're getting a ten thousand dollar reward?"

Sly nodded. "Yep. Personally. A check made out to me."

It was after school. Robin and his friends, including Chantelle, had come to the Center to meet up with Mr. Smith and share the good news about Sly's reward. Chantelle had never been to the Center, so the kids introduced her to everyone. She was welcomed like family.

Now they were together with Mr. Smith in the Center's lobby. They could hear the sound of jazz being played on a piano in the social hall. Robin knew that it had to be Wanda at the keyboard.

"Whatchu gonna do with that money?" Mr. Smith asked.

That was a good question. Robin had decided he wouldn't blame Sly if he kept it. Sly's dream was to be rich and famous; ten grand could go a long way toward getting started.

"He's giving it to the church for the mission," Chantelle declared.

"I am?" Sly asked.

"Of course you are!" Kaykay jumped in to back up Chantelle. "You didn't earn it, Sly. Robin found that chop shop. All you did was make the call. Besides, you're part of the group. Robin in da hood. We take from the bad and give to the good! Uh-huh!" Kaykay popped a few moves that made everyone grin.

"What if I don't want to give it to the good? What if I want to keep it?" Sly asked them. "I mean, I'm jus' askin'."

Chantelle leaned over and kissed Sly on the cheek. "That'll be the first and last kiss you get from me. But if you give the money to the church, who knows?"

"Done deal," Sly pronounced.

"Smart boy," Chantelle told him. She didn't kiss him again, but she slid over next to him and took his hand in hers. Sly grinned from ear to ear.

*She likes him. And as more than just a friend.*

Kaykay edged toward Robin. "I don't want you to feel left out." She kissed Robin on the cheek and took his hand.

"How about Mr. Smith?" Robin asked.

The two girls looked at each other. Then, as if they'd planned it, they stepped toward

Mr. Smith, stood on tiptoes, and kissed him too—one on each cheek.

Mr. Smith grinned as big as Sly had. "That's all the reward I need."

Robin held up one finger. "Now that the kissing is done, can I have everyone's attention?"

Everyone quieted. Robin thought for a moment about what he wanted to say, exactly.

"Well, we got the money for the church mission," he told them. "Not the way we planned, but we got it anyway. I'm thinking that maybe this is a sign. Maybe Robin in da hood really does need to get back in business."

"We already in business!" Sly shouted.

"I mean, against the Rangers. There's a lot of good we can do, and a lot of ways we can do it. As long as we use our heads." He took a long look at Chantelle. "I'm counting on you here," Robin said seriously.

"I won't let you down, Robin. Or any of you," Chantelle promised.

Sly whooped. "Robin in da hood be a hun'red percent back!"

Robin laughed. His ace, Sly, was right. Robin in da hood was a "hun'red percent back."

He wanted to start by helping out the community clinic. That could only happen by planning their next operation.

"Gather in close," Robin told everyone. "I've got an idea."